An Extraordinary Ordinary Moth

By Karlin Gray & Illustrated by Steliyana Doneva

I'm an ordinary moth,
as you can plainly see.
A dusty, grayish, dull insect—
nothing-special me.

I'm nothing like the Luna Moth,
who floats in graceful green.

I'm nothing like the Spider Moth—
so cool at Halloween!

I can't hum like Hummingbird Moth,
who sips with her long tongue.

I can't hide like Wood Nymph Moth, disguised as birdy dung.

The Atlas is a massive moth—a GIANT of the skies.

And don't even get me started on beloved butterflies!

I'm not special like those guys.
They are extraordinary.
I'm a dusty, grayish moth—
very ordinary.

"A moth! A moth!"
a boy then screams.
He's running up to me.
I freeze and blend in with the wall.

Maybe he won't see.

But when his twinkling eyes shine bright...
his smile grows wide with pure delight....

His happy face is such a sight....

I move toward his joyful light.

Flying into his cupped hands, I hope I don't get hurt.
Humans always shoo me off and make me feel like dirt.

"EW, a BUG!"
his sister squeals,
and flicks his hands away.

I flip and flutter in the air

until I hear him say:

"Hey, it's an **INSECT**—not a bug—
and my favorite kind!"
He follows me all through the yard,
with her two steps behind.

"It's just a dusty moth." She shrugs.
"Nothing special there."
He shakes his head and reaches out.
"Well, that's not really fair!"

"He's not dusty—those are scales that keep him warm at night.

And they flake off in a web so he escapes all right."

"Hmm," she says. "But why's it gray?
That's just kind of blah."
"No, it's not," he says to her,
and looks at me with awe.

"It's camouflage so he can hide while resting in the day. At night he flies above the flowers, and moonlight guides his way."

"His antennae smell for miles—perfect for exploring."

Smiling down at me, he says,
"How can that be boring?!"

"Okay, okay, I guess he's cool."
Her eyes shine down on me.
Then she yells back toward their house:
"Hurry, come and see!"

Their mom steps out and asks the kids,
"So, what bug did you find?"
The girl says, "Mom—a moth's an insect,
and our favorite kind!"

So how 'bout THAT?!

I'm someone's FAVORITE!

Little, grayish me—

proof of how

EXTRAORDINARY

ordinary
can be.

10 EXTRAORDINARY Facts About Moths

1. Moths rule! There are ten to fifteen times more species of moths than butterflies in the world.

(Source: *Science Friday*, "'Moth-ers' Celebrate Less-Loved Lepidopterans," featuring Elena Tartaglia, cofounder of National Moth Week, https://www.sciencefriday.com/segments/ -moth-ers-celebrate-less-loved-lepidopterans/)

2. Moths aren't dusty—they're scaly: A moth's wings are made up of *thousands* of tiny scales that create their patterns and colors. When a moth flutters into a spiderweb, its scales detach so the moth can fly away.

(Sources: Butterfly Conservation, "What Are Moths?," http://www.mothscount.org/text/15/what_are_moths_.html; *Virginia Quarterly Review*, "Scales: On the Wings of Butterflies and Moths," http://www.vqronline.org/vqr-portfolio/scales-wings-butterflies-and-moths)

3. Moths are ancient: Moths have been around for 195 million years; Homo sapiens (humans) have been around for only about 200,000 years.

(Sources: American Museum of Natural History blog, https://www.amnh.org/explore/news-blogs/news-posts/happy-national-moth-week!; Smithsonian National Museum of Natural History, http://humanorigins.si.edu/evidence/human-fossils/species/homo-sapiens)

4. Moths are master impersonators: Through evolution, some moths mimic other animals or objects, scaring off predators. The Wood Nymph looks like bird poop, and the Spider Moth looks like, well, a spider!

(Sources: Butterflies and Moths of America, https://www.butterfliesandmoths.org/species/Eudryas-grata; Business Insider, "Silly Moth, You Aren't a Spider," http://www.businessinsider. com/lygodium-spider-moth-pictures-2013-4)

5. Moths can be pollinators: At night, moths have an easier time finding fragrant and light-colored flowers to pollinate. Although some moths, like the Hummingbird Moth, pollinate flowers during the day.

(Source: United States Department of Agriculture Forest Service, https://www.fs.fed.us/wildflowers/pollinators/pollinator-of-the-month/hummingbird_moth.shtml, https://www.fs.fed.us/ wildflowers/pollinators/animals/moths.shtml)

6. Even without noses, moths are expert sniffers: A moth's antennae are made up of smell receptors that can detect the odor molecules of another moth from miles away.

(Source: *The Q? Blog*, a blog by Q?rius, a Smithsonian National Museum of Natural History website, "Hey Moth, That's a Great Rack on Your Head," http://qrius.si.edu/blog/hey-moth-thats-great-rack-your-head)

7. Moths are mysterious: Why are moths attracted to light? No one knows for sure, but there are several theories. One is that moths confuse artificial light with the moonlight that they use to navigate. Another is that they mistake the wavelengths of flames with those of female moths. Why do you think moths are attracted to light?

(Sources: The Lepidopterists' Society, Frequently Asked Questions #18, https://www.lepsoc.org/content/frequently-asked-questions#18; Science Focus, "Why are moths attracted to lights?," http://www.sciencefocus.com/qa/why-are-moths-attracted-lights)

8. Moths are celebrated around the world: Butterflies have a national day, but moths are celebrated for seven days during National Moth Week! To learn more, visit www.nationalmothweek.org.

9. Moths are different from butterflies: Butterflies have knobbed antennae; smooth, slender bodies; and they fly during the day. Moths have straight or feathery antennae; plump and fuzzy bodies; and they generally fly at night. When resting, butterflies hold their wings upright, while moths flatten out their wings.

(Sources: The Field Museum, Butterfly Basics, Butterflies vs. Moths, http://archive.fieldmuseum.org/butterfly/bvsm_basic.htm)

10. Moths are insects—not bugs: A "bug" is defined as belonging to the order *Hemiptera*. Moths and butterflies belong to the order *Lepidoptera* (meaning "scale wing"), which are insects. If you grow up to be a scientist who studies moths, you will be a lepidopterist!

(Source: Arizona State University School of Life Sciences, Ask a Biologist, "True Bugs," https://askabiologist.asu.edu/explore/true-bugs)

Disclaimer: Above website information (including links) was accessible and correct as of the publication date of this book.

 ACTIVITY

Observing moths can be as easy as turning your porch lights on and waiting to see what kind of moths show up. Or you could make a moth observation box:

Step 1: Put a battery-operated light source (like a lantern or flashlight) in a shoe box. No flames!

Step 2: Turn on the light source.

Step 3: Instead of putting the lid on, cover the box with plastic wrap or a white pillowcase.

Step 4: Place the box outside at night, away from any other lights. Position the box on its side.

Step 5: Check the box periodically to see if any moths have landed on your observation box.

Step 6: Take photos of any moths and share them with your friends.

For GGS—who taught me how to see the extraordinary in the ordinary

–KG

🐝

To my son, Bogomil, who loves all the small critters on Earth

–SD

Sleeping Bear Press
2395 South Huron Parkway, Suite 200
Ann Arbor, MI 48104
www.sleepingbearpress.com

Printed and bound in China.

10 9 8 7 6 5 4 3 2 1

Library of Congress Cataloging-in-Publication Data

Names: Gray, Karlin, author. | Doneva, Steliyana, illustrator.
Title: An extraordinary ordinary moth / written by Karlin Gray ; illustrated by Steliyana Doneva.
Description: Ann Arbor, MI : Sleeping Bear Press, 2017.
Identifiers: LCCN 2017029813 | ISBN 9781585363728
Subjects: LCSH: Moths—Juvenile literature.
Classification: LCC QL544.2 .G738 2017 | DDC 595.78—dc23
LC record available at https://lccn.loc.gov/2017029813